ABOUT THE BANK STREET READY-TO-READ SERIES

Seventy years of educational research and innovative teaching have given the Bank Street College of Education the reputation as America's most trusted name in early childhood education.

Because no two children are exactly alike in their development, we have designed the *Bank Street Ready-to-Read* series in three levels to accommodate the individual stages of reading readiness of children ages four through eight.

○ *Level 1:* GETTING READY TO READ—read-alouds for children who are taking their first steps toward reading.

○ *Level 2:* READING TOGETHER—for children who are just beginning to read by themselves but may need a little help.

○ *Level 3:* I CAN READ IT MYSELF—for children who can read independently.

Our three levels make it easy to select the books most appropriate for a child's development and enable him or her to grow with the series step by step. The *Bank Street Ready-to-Read* books also overlap and reinforce each other, further encouraging the reading process.

We feel that making reading fun and enjoyable is the single most important thing that you can do to help children become good readers. And we hope you'll be a part of Bank Street's long tradition of learning through sharing.

The Bank Street College of Education

D0289700

To John-John
— W.H.H.
To Star, who is always ready
to patiently be a horrible
hound model for me
— C.N.

LITTLE POSS AND HORRIBLE HOUND

A Bantam Little Rooster Book/August 1992

Little Rooster is a trademark of Bantam Books,
a division of Bantam Doubleday Dell Publishing Group, Inc.

Series graphic design by Alex Jay/Studio J

Special thanks to James A. Levine, Betsy Gould,
Diane Arico, and Ron Puhalski.

Library of Congress Cataloging-in-Publication Data

Hooks, William H.
Little Poss and Horrible Hound/by William H. Hooks;
illustrated by Carol Newsom.
p. cm. — (Bank Street ready-to-read)
"A Byron Preiss book."
"A Bantam little rooster book."
Summary: Following his father's sage advice,
Little Poss narrowly escapes from Horrible Hound.
ISBN 0-553-07881-X. — ISBN 0-553-35161-3 (pbk.)
[1. Opossums — Fiction.   2. Fathers and sons — Fiction.
3. Conduct of life — Fiction.]   I. Newsom, Carol, ill.
II. Title.   III. Series.
PZ7.H7664Lj   1992
[E] — dc20
91-28586   CIP   AC

Published simultaneously in the United States and Canada

Bantam Books are published by Bantam Books, a division of Bantam Doubleday Dell
Publishing Group, Inc. Its trademark, consisting of the words "Bantam Books" and the
portrayal of a rooster, is Registered in U.S. Patent and Trademark Office and in other
countries. Marca Registrada. Bantam Books, 666 Fifth Avenue, New York, New York 10103.

PRINTED IN THE UNITED STATES OF AMERICA

0 9 8 7 6 5 4 3 2 1

Bank Street Ready-to-Read™

Little Poss and Horrible Hound

by William H. Hooks
Illustrated by Carol Newsom

A Byron Preiss Book

A BANTAM LITTLE ROOSTER BOOK
NEW YORK · TORONTO · LONDON · SYDNEY · AUCKLAND

Beware the Hound

Little Poss and Papa Possum
were sitting in the sweet gum tree.
''I saw Horrible Hound
in the woods today,'' said Little Poss.

4

"Bad news," said Papa Possum.
"Horrible Hound means trouble.
Do you remember
the Possum's Golden Rule?"
asked Papa Possum.
Little Poss looked puzzled.

"I'll tell you again," said Papa.
"Beware the Hound."
"What's a *beware*?" asked Little Poss.
"It means never let Horrible Hound
sneak up on you," said Papa Possum.

6

"I'll say it over and over,"
said Little Poss.
"Then I won't forget it."
Little Poss ran along a branch saying,
"Beware the hound!
Beware the hound!"

He ran so far out
that the branch snapped.
Down, down, Little Poss fell,
yelling, "Beware the hound!"

Just as Little Poss crashed down,
Horrible Hound was passing
under the sweet gum tree.

Horrible looked up.
He saw a flying possum
coming straight toward him,
yelling, "Beware the hound!"

Horrible tucked in his tail
and bolted out of the woods.
Little Poss landed on his feet,
as possums tend to do.
Then he climbed back up the tree.

Papa Possum looked worried.
But Little Poss said, "Now I know
what a *beware* really is."
"What?" asked Papa Possum.
"A *beware* is a good scare
that frightens the hound away!"
said Little Poss.

One a Day

Little Poss and Papa Poss
were eating and talking.
"May I have another persimmon?"
asked Little Poss.
"We *were* talking about
Horrible Hound," said Papa Possum.
But Little Poss was too hungry to listen.
"Just one more persimmon, please?"
he begged.

"A possum needs more than
persimmons to grow on," said Papa.
"Here, try one of these."
Papa threw Little Poss
a round, red thing.
"One a day keeps the doctor away,"
said Papa Possum.

14

Little Poss climbed down the tree
with the round, red thing.
It looked like a huge pill.
Who could swallow such a thing?
It was big enough to choke a hound.
''I'll hide it for now,'' said Little Poss.

He ran down the path
to the old hollow tree.
''I'll hide it here,'' he said.
Suddenly he heard a terrible noise.

It was Horrible Hound!
He was barking his
''I've-got-you-now!'' bark.

Little Poss was scared,
but he was thinking fast.
"You can't have my magic pill,"
he said.
"What magic pill?" asked Horrible.

Little Poss said quickly,
"One a day keeps the doctor away!"
"I hate doctors,"
snapped Horrible Hound.
"Give me that magic pill,
or I'll eat you up right now."

Little Poss reached
into the hollow tree.

He pulled out the round, red thing.
"You have to close your eyes
and say the magic words three times,
or the pill won't work."
"What magic words?" asked Horrible.
Little Poss said, "You have to say,
'One a day keeps the doctor away!'"

"Then hurry up," growled Horrible.
Little Poss popped the big, red thing
into Horrible Hound's mouth.
"Now close your eyes," said Little Poss,
"and say the magic words three times."

"I forgot the words,"
mumbled Horrible.
Little Poss said,
"One a day keeps the doctor away!"

Horrible Hound closed his eyes and
mumbled the magic words.
Little Poss ran down the path.

Horrible Hound mumbled again.
By this time, Little Poss had
reached the sweet gum tree.

Horrible mumbled the magic
words a third time,
"One a day keeps the doctor away!"
By the time Horrible had said
the magic words three times,
Little Poss was back up the tree.

"Your cheeks look pink already,"
said Papa Possum.
"I told you," Papa said,
"an apple a day
keeps the doctor away!"
Little Poss smiled and said,
"I want an apple every day."

"That's my Little Poss," said Papa.
"Apples are good for you."
"I know," said Little Poss.
Then he said to himself,
"An apple a day
keeps the hound away!"

If Wishes Were Wings

Little Poss was watching Bumble Bee.
Bumble circled and soared in the air.
"If only I could fly," cried Poss,
"Horrible Hound would
never catch me!"

"Don't be silly," said Papa Possum.
"Who ever heard of a flying possum?"
"I wish I could anyway," said Poss.
"Listen carefully," said Papa.
"I'll tell you an old possum saying."

Papa said in a deep, wise voice,
"If wishes were wings,
possums would fly."
Little Poss nodded his head,
but he didn't understand.

"Now run along and play.
Forget about this flying business.
And watch out for Horrible Hound."
Little Poss ran along singing
the wise possum saying.
He sang it over and over.

"If wishes were wings,
possums would fly!
If wishes were wings,
possums would fly!

If wishes were wings,
possums would fly!''
Little Poss finished the song with
"Flap your wings, my possum!"

PLOP!
He landed on top of a big ball
of white and brown fur.
It was Horrible Hound,
curled up and asleep.

Horrible Hound's eyes popped open.
He grabbed Little Poss!

Little Poss was so frightened,
he said,
"If wishes were wings,
possums would fly!"

Horrible Hound growled,
"If wishes were possums,
I'd eat one every day!"
Little Poss was scared,
but he was thinking fast.
"I know a big secret," he cried.

"A secret? Tell me," said Horrible,
"or I'll eat you up right now!"
"I know how to fly," said Little Poss.
"Show me!" growled Horrible Hound.

"With your beautiful long tail
and your big floppy ears,
you could fly right away,"
said Little Poss.
"Show me!" growled Horrible again.

"All you have to do," said Poss,
"is tie your tail to your back legs,
flap your ears three times, and shout,
'If wishes were wings,
hounds would fly!'"

"Quick, tie my tail around my legs,"
snapped Horrible Hound.
Little Poss jumped
out of Horrible's paws.
He quickly tied Horrible's long tail
around his back legs.

"Now flap your ears," said Poss,
"and we'll say together,
'If wishes were wings,
hounds would fly!'"

Horrible Hound said the words.
But he did not fly.
He was trapped with his tail
tied around his legs.
He barked and bounced around
on the rocky ground.

Little Poss rushed back
to the sweet gum tree.
Papa Possum cried,
"You had me worried, Poss.
What were you doing?"
"Nothing," said Little Poss.
"I was just playing."

"Oh," said Papa Possum.
"I thought you might be trying
that silly flying business."
"No," said Little Poss.
"I remember what you said."
"Good possum," said Papa.
"Wishes and wings
are not possum things."

"Maybe not," said Little Poss.
"But there's something
this possum can do."
"What?" asked Papa Possum.
Little Poss smiled and said,
"Use my head instead!"